A LITTLE SPOT WEARS A MASK

To my children, Ryan and Anna

This book belongs to:

_____

_____

_____

There is a virus going around that is making some people very sick, so we need to wear MASKS to help prevent the virus from spreading. Since this virus can spread without people feeling sick, wearing MASKS can help protect everyone!

How do MASKS help?

When you sneeze or cough, droplets fly out of your nose or mouth.

These droplets have germs in them and can travel 6 feet...the length of your bed!

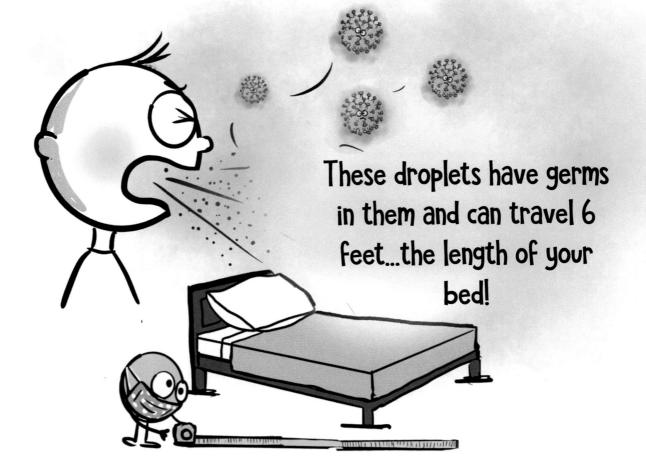

Not all germs are bad, but if germs contain a virus, they can make people very sick. Some viruses are very contagious, which means they can spread quickly to other people and make them sick.

That is why it is so important to cough or sneeze in your elbow and wash your hands! But sometimes that isn't enough, so we need to add an extra layer of protection.

That's where MASKS can help!
A MASK can block some of the germs
from traveling!

For a MASK to work
best, it needs to cover your
nose and mouth, because that's where
the germs come in and out!

There is also a right way to PUT ON a MASK.

Let me show you!

The first thing to remember is to WASH your hands
BEFORE putting on a MASK...

and AFTER taking it off!

Okay, now let's learn how to put it ON!

The next step when putting on a MASK, is to ONLY touch the loops. Try to avoid touching the fabric part of the MASK because that is where the most germs are found.

Step One:
Hold the MASK
by the loops!

Step Two:
Bring the MASK
to your face and
place the loops over
your ears!

Woo Hoo!
You did it!

When taking off a MASK, ONLY grab the loops!
Remember, the fabric part of the MASK can have germs.

Step One:
Carefully remove the loop over one ear.

Step Two:
While holding the other side, remove the loop over your other ear.

You did it!

Now make sure you put it in a safe place!

A safe place to store MASKS
are little plastic bags.

Bring a few extra CLEAN MASKS
to school, in case they
get dirty! Also, make sure to
wash your reusable MASKS at
home after you wear them!

A common way a MASK can get dirty
is when you sneeze! This is a perfect time
to change your mask!

Even though you are wearing a MASK, you should still cover your
mouth with your elbow for extra protection.

At lunch or during snack time, you will need to remove your MASK to eat.

Once you remove your MASK, be sure to put it in a safe place and wash your hands!

Then after you eat, wash your hands and put your MASK back on.

Now that you know HOW TO WEAR A MASK, it's time to have a little FUN! I know MASKS can feel a little funny at first, so I have some tips to make them more comfortable!

You can pick out your own fabric!

There are so many styles and colors! You can even use some clothing you already have, like a bandana!

Have an adult help you find breathable fabric
to make into a MASK.

GET CREATIVE!

You can decorate a clean MASK with crayons or markers!

Use your
IMAGINATION!

Using MASKS when you play, is a great
way to get used to wearing and seeing MASKS!

You could be a superhero or a veterinarian!

Take funny photos with your MASK on!

Ask your family and friends to send pictures of themselves in MASKS, too!

The more you see and wear MASKS, the more comfortable they will become!

Okay! Now
it's time to practice!
Put on your mask!

Now take
it off!

YOU ARE DOING
AMAZING!

Now try to
put on and take off
your mask 5 times
in a row!

I am so PROUD of you! I hope these
tips can help WEARING a MASK easier!
I can't wait to see what MASK you
are going to wear to school!

Also available:

A Little SPOT Stays Home and *A Little SPOT Learns Online* are companions to *A Little SPOT Wears A Mask*. These stories help children understand viruses and why it is important to stay home when you are sick and what to expect when learning online.

For free printables and worksheets that go along with these books, visit www.dianealber.com

Made in the USA
Middletown, DE
19 August 2020

15493527R00020